What's the time, GRANDMA

STAFFORDSHIRE LIBRARY AND INFORMATION SERVICES
Please return or renew by the last date shown

TAM	JUN 08	
Tamworth Junior Library 01827 475645	25. JUN 08	
	09. JUL	
	26. JUN 08	
16. DEC 08	30. AUG 08	
21. 05. 07	02. SEP 08	
	OCT 08	
09 JUN 07	Tamworth Junior Library	
28. JUL 07	0300 111 8000	
	2 3 MAR 2022	
	2 4 NOV 2022	
13. AUG 07		
SEP 07		
19. MAY 08		

If not required by other readers, this item may be renewed
in person, by post or telephone, online or by email.
To renew, either the book or ticket are required.

24 HOUR RENEWAL LINE - 0845 33 00 740

D0412139

for Janet and Gerald

STAFFORDSHIRE LIBRARIES ARTS AND ARCHIVES	
38014041155166	
PET	03-Aug-06
CF	£5.99
TAMW	

Copyright ©2001 by Ken Brown.
This paperback edition first published in 2003 by Andersen Press Ltd.
The rights of Ken Brown to be identified as the author and illustrator of this work
have been asserted by him in accordance with the Copyright, Designs and Patents Act, 1988.
First published in Great Britain in 2001 by Andersen Press Ltd. 20 Vauxhall Bridge Road, London SW1V 2SA.
Published in Australia by Random House Australia Pty., 20 Alfred Street, Milsons Point, Sydney, NSW 2061.
All rights reserved. Colour separated in Switzerland by Photolitho AG, Zurich.
Printed and bound in Italy by Grafiche AZ, Verona.

10 9 8 7 6 5 4 3

British Library Cataloguing in Publication Data available.

ISBN 1 84270 068 5

This book has been printed on acid-free paper

What's the time, GRANDMA WOLF?

Ken Brown

Andersen Press

London

There's a wolf in the woods
and everyone said:
    "She's big and she's bad, she's old
      and she's hairy. Best leave her alone,
      she's SCARY!"

But we wanted to know,

so we crept a bit closer . . .

and Piglet, who's brave,
shouted . . .

"WHAT'S THE TIME, GRANDMA WOLF?"
  And she opened her eyes –
they were very, very big –
and yawned, "It's time I got up."

So we crept a bit closer and Fawn, who is shy,
whispered: "What's the time, Grandma Wolf?"
And she pricked up her ears –
they were very, very big – and said,
"It's time I cleaned my teeth."

So we crept a bit closer and Crow,
who is noisy, squawked: "What's the
time, Grandma Wolf?"
And she took down a cauldron –
it was very, very big – and said,
"It's time I scrubbed the stewpot."

So we crept a bit closer and Squirrel, who's saucy, squeaked: "What's the time, Grandma Wolf?"

And she fetched a sharp axe – it was very, very big – and said, "It's time to chop the wood."

So we crept a bit closer and Badger,
who's bold, barked: "What's the time, Grandma Wolf?"
    And she picked up two pails –
they were very, very big – and said,
"It's time I fetched some water."

So we crept a bit closer and Duckling, who's daft, quacked: "What's the time, Grandma Wolf?"

And she looked down her nose –
it was very, very big – and said,
"It's time to light the fire!"

So we crept even closer and Rabbit, who's reckless, giggled: "What's the time, Grandma Wolf . . . ?"

So we all settled down to
a vegetable stew, and old
Grandma Wolf, what did she do?

She read us our
favourite story!

More Andersen Press paperback picture books!

Ruggles
by Anne Fine and Ruth Brown

Betty's Not Well Today
by Gus Clarke

The Great Castle of Marshmangle
by Malachy Doyle and Paul Hess

War and Peas
by Michael Foreman

Zebra's Hiccups
by David McKee

The Wrong Overcoat
by Hiawyn Oram and Mark Birchall

Super Dooper Jezebel
by Tony Ross

Bear's Eggs
by Dieter and Ingrid Schubert

Rabbit's Wish
by Paul Stewart and Chris Riddell

Mr Bear and the Bear
by Frances Thomas and Ruth Brown

Frog and a Very Special Day
by Max Velthuijs

What Did I Look Like When I Was a Baby?
by Jeanne Willis and Tony Ross